This Topsy and Tim
book belongs to

# Theo

All Ladybird books are available at most bookshops, supermarkets
and newsagents, or can be ordered direct from:
**Ladybird Postal Sales** PO Box 133 Paignton TQ3 2YP England
*Telephone:* (+44) 01803 554761 *Fax:* (+44) 01803 663394
A catalogue record for this book is available from the British Library

Published by Ladybird Books Ltd
A subsidiary of the Penguin Group
A Pearson Company

© Jean and Gareth Adamson MCMXCV
This edition MCMXCIX

The moral rights of the author/illustrator have been asserted
LADYBIRD and the device of a Ladybird are trademarks of Ladybird Books Ltd Loughborough Leicestershire UK

# people who help us stories

Jean and Gareth Adamson

# Contents

# go to the doctor

It was a cold and misty morning.
Mummy cooked a tasty hot breakfast
for Topsy and Tim.
'Don't want any breakfast,' said Tim.

'Oh, you are a misery,' said Mummy crossly.
Dad was not cross, but then, he had not
cooked the breakfast.
'This isn't like Tim,' he said.
'There must be something wrong.
Open your mouth wide, Tim.'
Tim's throat was swollen and red.
'Poor old Tim,' said Dad.

Mummy phoned the Health Centre.
She made an appointment for Tim
to see Dr Sims.
They walked to the Health Centre.
Tim wore his scarf up over his nose
to keep his sore throat warm.

The receptionist checked Tim's appointment in her big book. She told them to go and wait outside Dr Sims' surgery.
'Look,' said Topsy. 'There's Kerry.'
Kerry was one of Topsy and Tim's school friends.

'What's the matter, Kerry?'
asked Topsy.
'It hurts when I swallow,'
Kerry said.
'Tim has a sore throat too,'
said Topsy.
Tim just looked glum.

Soon it was Tim's turn to go into
the surgery.
'Good morning,' said Dr Sims.
'Good morning, Dr Sims,' said Topsy.
Tim said nothing.

'Tim isn't talking,'
Topsy explained.
'I think it's because
his throat hurts.'

'Open your mouth, Tim,' said Dr Sims,
'and let me see.'
Dr Sims took a little flat stick
and held it on Tim's tongue.
'Say Ah,' he said.

Then he looked at Tim's eyes
and inside his ears.
'You must have bad ear-ache
too, Tim,' he said.
Tim nodded.
'You're a brave lad,'
said Dr Sims.

'Mmm,' said Dr Sims. 'Up with your jumper,
young man.'
He put his stethoscope into his ears
and listened to Tim's chest.

'That looks like a telephone,' said Tim.
'Yes,' said Dr Sims. 'I can hear
what chests and tummies are saying
through it. The sound tells me
if people are ill.'
Then he let Topsy listen to Tim's
heart beating.

Dr Sims wrote a prescription and gave it
to Mummy. 'One spoonful four times a day,'
he said. 'This will soon make you feel
better, Tim.'

Mrs White, the dispenser, prepared Tim's medicine and gave it to Mummy.
'Make sure he takes all the medicine,' she said.

**Dispensary**

Mummy put the medicine safely in her bag.
Just then, Kerry came past.
'I've got some medicine,' she said.
'Tim's got some too,' said Topsy.

When they got home, Mummy took out the medicine. It had a special childproof top, but Mummy could open it. She poured out a spoonful for Tim.
'Did it taste nice?' asked Topsy.
'Mmm,' said Tim, licking his lips.

Then Mummy locked the bottle of medicine
away in a cupboard, out of Topsy and
Tim's reach.

When Dad came home, Tim was tucking into
blackcurrant jelly. Topsy was not eating hers.
'She's sulking because she isn't ill,'
said Tim.
'I wonder,' said Dad. 'Open wide,
Topsy, and let Dr Dad have a look.'
Topsy's throat was red and sore.

Dad took Topsy to the Health Centre that evening. Her throat was sore but she was proud to be going to see the doctor.

Dr Sims was not there, so Topsy saw
Dr Jaunty instead. She came home
with a bottle of medicine just like Tim's.